Circle C Beginnings

Andi's Pony Trouble

Susan K. Marlow
Illustrated by Leslie Gammelgaard

Kregel
Publications

Andi's Pony Trouble
©2010 by Susan K. Marlow

Illustrations ©2010 by Leslie Gammelgaard

Published by Kregel Publications, a division of Kregel, Inc.,
P.O. Box 2607, Grand Rapids, MI 49501.

The persons and events portrayed in this work are the creations
of the author, and any resemblance to persons living or dead is
purely coincidental.

Library of Congress Cataloging-in-Publication Data
Marlow, Susan K.
    Andi's pony trouble / Susan K. Marlow ; illustrated by
Leslie Gammelgaard.
        p. cm. — (Circle C beginnings series ; [1])
    [1. Ranch life—California—Fiction. 2. Ponies—Fiction.
3. Horses—Fiction. 4. Growth—Fiction. 5. Family life—
California—Fiction. 6. California—History—1850-1950—
Fiction.] I. Gammelgaard, Leslie, ill. II. Title.
    PZ7.M34528Amp   2010   [Fic]—dc22   2010033381

ISBN 978-0-8254-4181-3

Printed in the United States of America
12 13 14 15 / 6 5 4

Contents

New Words

britches	pants
cattle	cows
coop	a place where chickens are kept
corral	a fenced-in place to keep horses
foal	a baby horse
howdy	hi
lope	to run faster than a trot but not as fast as a gallop
ranch	a farm where people raise cattle and horses
roundup	when cowboys gather up the cattle to sell them
whinny	a sound a horse makes

Chapter 1

Andi's Big Idea

Andi Carter dropped her spoon into her empty bowl. "I have something to say."

Her family kept right on talking.

Andi looked around the breakfast table. She knew that children with good manners did not talk during meals. Polite children waited until somebody talked to them.

But the only time somebody talked to Andi at the table was when they said, "Pass the salt, Andi."

That was not talking. That was bossing.

"I have something to say," Andi said a little bit louder.

Nobody was listening.

Andi felt grumpy. Being the little sister was not fair. Her three big brothers talked at the table. They talked about cows and horses and roundups. Andi's big sister Melinda was eleven years old. She sometimes talked at the table, but mostly she giggled.

And that's worse than talking, Andi thought.

Andi couldn't wait one minute longer. She had something to say, and she was going to say it.

Even if it wasn't polite.

"I have something to say!" she yelled.

That got her family's attention, but not in a good way.

"Andrea!" Mother said. Her eyes opened wide, like she was surprised. "Are you shouting at the table?"

Of course I'm shouting. How else can anybody hear me? Andi thought. But she did not say those words out loud. That's what Mother called "talking back."

Andi did not like what happened to her when she talked back.

"I'm sorry, Mother," she said quickly, before everybody started talking again. "I have to tell you something."

"What is it, Andi?" Justin asked. "It must be important." He smiled at her. Justin always smiled at her. Even when she was acting grumpy.

Andi loved her oldest brother.

"It *is* important!" She looked around. Now nobody was talking. Everybody was waiting for Andi to talk. At last!

She smiled. "It's very, *very* important."

"Well, what is it?" Andi's brother Chad asked. He sounded like he was in a hurry—like always. He probably wanted to talk about cows and horses and ranch work some more.

Andi scowled at Chad. She wanted to stick her tongue out at him, but she didn't do it. That would not be good table manners.

Instead, she looked at Mother. "I have decided that I'm too big to ride my pony. I want a horse of my own."

Nobody said a word.

Then Chad laughed. "When did you hatch this silly idea?"

"It's not a silly idea," Andi said. "And I didn't hatch it. Ideas don't get hatched. Chicks get hatched. From eggs."

Andi knew this was true. There were lots of fuzzy, yellow baby chicks on the ranch. They all hatched from eggs.

"Chad," Mother said in her warning voice. It meant, *Don't tease your sister.*

Andi was glad Mother said that. Chad teased her so much that sometimes she wanted

to punch him. But he was too big and too quick. Every time she went after him, Chad grabbed her and held her upside down until she got tired of trying to hit him.

And he always laughed.

"I'm sorry, Andi," Chad said. "What makes you think you're big enough for a horse?"

Andi gave Chad a big smile and pointed to the calendar. "I have been thinking about this ever since the calendar changed to M-A-Y 1-8-7-4."

Andi could not read, but she knew all her letters and numbers. "My birthday is this month. I'm going be six years old. I'm much too big to keep riding Coco."

Melinda giggled. Like always.

"You're not big enough," her brother Mitch said. He stood up and lifted Andi from her chair. "Look here. You hardly come up past my belt. You can walk under a horse's belly without bending over."

Everybody laughed. Everybody but Andi.

She crossed her arms and looked up at Mitch. "I am *too* big enough. I can show you."

Andi walked out of the dining room and

into the kitchen. She did not walk ladylike. She stomped just a little bit.

"Where are you going?" Mother asked.

Andi poked her head through the doorway. "Come and see."

Chapter 2

Big Enough?

Andi ducked back in the kitchen and waited. Her heart was thumping fast. Pretty soon she would not be riding that pokey old pony any more. No, sir! This was one of her best ideas ever.

"When Mother sees how big I am, she'll let me have a horse. I know she will," Andi told herself.

Melinda ran into the kitchen giggling. "What are you going to show us, Andi?"

Andi rolled her eyes at giggle-box Melinda.

As soon as Mother and the boys came into the kitchen, Andi skipped across the room. Then she pointed to the wall next to the wood

Justin
Chad
MITCH
Melinda
Justin
Andi
Mitch
Justin
Chad
Andi
Melinda
Mitch
Andi

box. "Right there. That will show you I'm big enough."

Everybody looked.

Up and down the wall were lines with names next to them: Justin, Chad, Mitch, Melinda, and Andi. Mother drew a new line each year until the children stopped growing. In a few weeks, Mother would draw a new line for Andi.

"Watch!" Andi said.

Quick as a wink, she ran to the wall and backed up. She put her hand on her head and pushed it against the wall. Then she stepped away. "See? See how much I grew this year?"

Justin bent down to take a closer look. "Well! It sure does look like you've grown."

Andi smiled. She knew she was really close to getting a horse of her own. If Justin said she had grown, then it must be true.

She looked at Mother. "I would like a golden horse, Mother. A horse as shiny as a gold piece." She dug around in her pocket for her special coin.

Andi kept all kinds of treasures in her pockets: grasshoppers and string and marbles and rocks. She never knew when something in her pocket might come in handy. If she saw a snake, she could throw a rock at it. Or she could give it a grasshopper to eat. Then the snake would go away.

Maybe.

Andi pulled out a shiny gold coin and held it up. It was her Christmas coin. She found it in her stocking last Christmas.

"See?" she said. "I want a horse just this color."

Before Mother could answer, Chad said, "Not so fast, Andi. You can't be that tall. Go stand next to the wall again."

Andi did not want to do what bossy Chad said.

Sometimes her brother acted like he was *too big for his britches*. Andi heard the ranch boss tell her friend Riley that a lot. "You're too big for your britches, boy," he'd say.

Eight-year-old Riley was always acting too big for his britches.

Andi frowned. But then she did what Chad told her. She put her special coin in her pocket and backed up against the wall. She guessed it didn't hurt to show everybody how big she was—one more time.

Chad put his hand on her head.

Melinda giggled. "You're standing on your tiptoes, Andi. You can't do that."

Andi looked down at her feet. "Why not? Standing on my tiptoes makes me bigger. I have to be big so I can get a horse."

Chad slowly pushed down on Andi's head until she was standing on her flat feet. "Sorry, baby sister. That's not how it works."

"Don't call me that," Andi huffed. He always called her baby sister. "I'm not a baby."

"No, you're not," Mother said. She gave Chad one of those warning looks again. "But you are not quite ready for a horse. Coco is big enough for you right now."

Andi let out a big breath. Coco was an old, slow, worn-out pony. He wasn't even Andi's very own pony! Coco was everybody's pony. Even tall, grown-up Justin rode Coco when he was a little boy.

Andi did not want to ride a hand-me-down pony anymore.

"Coco is too old," she said. "He's like a great-grandpa pony. He only walks and trots."

"Which is just right for a little girl," Justin said.

19

Andi felt a tiny bit sick inside. Her tiptoe idea had not turned out too well. On her flat feet, Andi was little.

Too little.

"Please?" Andi said. Saying please sometimes helped.

But not this time.

"I'm sorry, Andrea," Mother said, "but you are not ready for a horse."

Andi slumped down on the floor.

It didn't look like she was going to get a horse this morning, after all.

Chapter 3

Chickens and Chores

After Andi's brothers and sister left the kitchen, Mother said, "Come here, sweetheart."

Andi didn't want to. She wanted to sit on the floor and feel sorry for herself. She wanted to think of a way to talk her mother into giving her a horse.

But she had to obey.

Mother was sitting in a chair. She lifted Andi onto her lap and gave her a hug. It felt good.

"There's more to having a horse than just being big enough," she said.

Andi wrinkled her eyebrows. "Like what?"

"Like taking care of a horse," Mother

explained. "Sometimes you forget to give Coco his hay. Then Chad and Mitch have to do it."

Andi looked at her lap. Why did Mother have to bring that up? Andi only forgot to feed Coco when she was busy doing other things.

Mother had more to say. "When was the last time you brushed Coco?"

Andi's shoulders went up and down. "I don't remember."

"And what about the time you left him tied up in the yard all day?"

Andi squirmed. That had not been a good day. Chad had yelled and yelled when he saw Coco tied up in the hot sun.

But Andi wasn't ready to give up yet.

"Father would give me a horse," she said softly, "if he were here instead of in Heaven."

Mother gave Andi an extra-warm hug. "I'm sure he would," she agreed, "just as soon as you were old enough to take care of one. But for now, Father would tell you that a pony is just right."

She lifted Andi off her lap and stood up. That meant the talking was over.

No horse today.

She blinked away a tear. "Yes, Mother."

Mother handed Andi the egg basket.

Chore time.

"I want you to be extra careful today when you gather the eggs," Mother said. "Do not swing the basket around in the air. Do not run with a full basket. Do not try to juggle the eggs."

Andi's sad face turned smiley. "Mitch can juggle four eggs at a time without breaking them."

"I know," Mother said. "But *you* may not juggle them. I don't want to see any broken eggs today."

"Yes, Mother." Andi took the basket, ran out the back door, and jumped off the porch. She skipped across the yard, all the way to the chicken coop.

Then she stopped.

Dozens of brown, black, and red chickens were looking at Andi from behind the chicken-wire fence. They were making cackling noises.

All night the chickens stayed safe in their coop. Now they wanted out. They wanted to run around the yard and catch bugs all day.

But nobody had opened the gate this
morning.

It was not Andi's job to let the chickens out.
It was her job to collect the eggs. She had to
walk through the coop and into the henhouse
to do it.

Andi did not want to go in there with all those chickens. Mostly she didn't want to go into the chicken coop with Henry the Eighth there. She saw him in a corner, scratching at the ground with his big, sharp feet.

"You mean old rooster," she said.

Henry looked up and made a warning noise in his throat.

Andi's heart thumped. She was not afraid of anything on the ranch. Not the cattle. Not the bull. Not even the wild horses when they snorted and bucked.

But she was afraid of that old rooster. He was big and shiny black, with colorful tail feathers. He had sharp claws on his feet. And he could run fast.

Andi did not like Henry the Eighth at all. Most of the time, she stayed far away from him.

But today he was right there in front of her.

Andi took a big breath. She had to get those eggs. So she opened the gate and stepped back as fast as she could.

The rooster and his hens raced out of the coop and into the yard.

Andi let out her breath. Henry had run

right past her. He was gone! Only three hens and their chicks had stayed behind in the coop. They were pecking in the dirt and did not look up when Andi walked by.

The henhouse was mostly empty too. Just two hens sat on their nests. One squawked when Andi poked her fingers under its fluffy body.

"Sorry, little red hen," she said. "Mother needs your egg." She found the rest of the eggs and slipped them into her basket.

"Sixteen . . . seventeen . . . eighteen." Andi counted the eggs.

She hurried out of the henhouse, but she did not run. She did not want to break any eggs today.

Andi started across the chicken coop to the open gate. Then she stopped.

Henry the Eighth was blocking her way.

Chapter 4

Riley to the Rescue

"Go away, you mean old rooster," Andi said. She tried to sound brave, but her hands felt shaky.

Henry the Eighth must have come back to take care of the hens and their chicks.

Andi was trapped.

Henry made a low, scary noise in his throat.

Andi felt shivers go up and down her arms. "Go away," she told Henry again. "Shoo!"

The rooster did not go away. He looked at Andi with his beady black eyes. He rose up high on his feet and flapped his wings.

Andi knew what would happen next. It had happened before. That big, mean rooster would chase her. He would peck her and scratch her.

She would spill her basket of eggs. It would be terrible!

Then Andi heard a shout.

"Run, Andi!"

It was her friend Riley. He was holding a big stick in his hand. He ran into the chicken coop, swinging the stick. "I'll take care of Henry," he yelled. "Run!"

Andi ran. She ran out of that coop as fast as she could go.

But she didn't get far. The rooster zigzagged away from Riley and went after Andi.

Andi screamed and ran faster.

Then something terrible happened. Andi tripped and fell. The eggs flew everywhere.

Crack! Two eggs broke on her head. Three more hit her on her arms and legs. The rest of the eggs fell to the ground. *Splat! Splat! Splat!*

And Henry was getting closer.

Riley raced over and hit the rooster with the stick. "Get out of here!" He swung at Henry again.

The rooster squawked. Then he turned and ran back to his hens.

Riley put down the stick. He looked at Andi and his eyes got big. He didn't say a word.

Andi sat in the dirt. She didn't say a word either. Drippy egg yolks and egg whites trickled down her face. They landed with a *plop* in her lap.

For a whole minute Andi and Riley stared at each other without talking.

"Thanks, Riley," Andi said at last.

"You look funny," Riley said. "It looks like

a chicken laid an egg on your head." He started laughing.

Andi was glad Riley had saved her from the rooster, but she didn't feel like laughing. It was not funny. What would Mother say? She told Andi to be extra careful this morning.

No broken eggs today, Andi!

But now it looked like all of the eggs were broken.

Andi saw her egg basket a few feet away. It was tipped over on its side. She crawled over to it and looked inside. Three brown eggs were left. One was cracked. That meant two eggs had not broken. Only two!

Uh-oh.

"Can you see any good eggs on the ground?" Andi asked. She really hoped there were more than two unbroken eggs left.

Riley shook his head. "Nope. They're all broken and mixed in with the dirt." He made a face. "You're mixed in with the dirt too. Maybe I should whistle for one of the dogs to come and clean it up."

Andi jumped to her feet. It was bad enough

to be covered with drippy eggs. She did not want the dogs licking her. *Yuck!*

"This is a really bad day," she told Riley. "I thought I was going to get my own horse, but Mother said I'm not big enough. Then she said I have to take better care of Coco. And *then* she told me to be extra careful with the eggs."

"Well," Riley said, "the day can't get much worse."

But Riley was wrong. All of a sudden, the day *did* get worse.

Chad and two other men came around the corner of the barn. They were leading their horses and talking. When they saw Andi and Riley they stopped short.

Chad's eyebrows went up, like he was very surprised.

"Howdy, Chad," Andi said in a tiny voice. "The eggs broke."

Chad didn't say anything right away. He looked like he was trying not to laugh. Then he pointed a finger at Riley. "You're the cook's helper, right?"

Riley nodded.

"Then go help him."

Riley took off running toward the cookhouse.

"And you," Chad said to Andi, "go ask Mother to clean you up before every egg-loving dog on this ranch gets to you first."

Andi grabbed her basket and ran to the house. She didn't look back, but she could hear her brother laughing.

Chapter 5

Slow-poke Pony

Andi sat on the back porch. Her hands and face were clean, but her head hurt. Mother had to scrub extra hard to get all the slimy egg mess out of her hair.

"I wish Melinda was home," Andi said. She put her chin in her hands and let out a big sigh.

Melinda was a giggle-box, but a big sister was good to have around on days like this. If Melinda were home, she would take Andi riding on Panda, her very own horse.

But Melinda was in school.

Andi stood up. It was no fun sitting around all by herself. "One . . . two . . . three . . ." She jumped off the porch. Porch steps were not made for going up and down. Porch steps were made for jumping off.

"Hey, Andi!" Riley called from across the yard. "Want to go riding with me?"

"I sure do!" Andi shouted back.

"I can ride for an hour," Riley said. "Then I have to carry firewood for Cook."

He ran off toward the small corral.

Andi hurried to catch up. "Do you like working all the time? Don't you wish you could play more?"

"Nope," Riley said. "I like working on a ranch. It's better than going to school. Lots better. Uncle Sid says I don't have to go back to school for a long time." He frowned. "Wait 'til you start school. You'll see what I mean."

Andi did not want to talk about school. Not ever.

"I see Midnight," she said to change the subject.

Midnight was Riley's big, black horse. He was fast—much faster than pokey old Coco. Andi rode Midnight lots of times. She never fell off, not even when she galloped as fast as the wind.

Andi climbed to the top of the rail fence and patted Midnight. "Howdy, Midnight."

Riley climbed up beside her. "Go get Coco so we can ride." He jumped inside the corral to be with his horse.

Andi looked at Riley and Midnight. No fair! She didn't want to ride Coco.

"Can I ride Midnight?" she asked.

"Not right now," Riley said. He grabbed Midnight's mane and pulled himself up on his horse. "Maybe later." He frowned. "Hurry up, Andi. Open the gate and go get Coco. I only have an hour."

Andi jumped down and opened the corral gate, but she wasn't happy.

"That bossy boy is acting too big for his britches," she said on her way to the barn. "Just because he's eight years old and has his own horse."

When Coco saw Andi, he gave a little whinny. He looked happy to see her.

Andi was not happy to see Coco. She found Coco's bridle and opened the door to his stall.

"Come on, you pokey, hand-me-down pony. Mother says I'm not ready for my own horse, so I guess I have to ride you."

Coco did not look like he cared that he was

a pokey, hand-me-down pony. He ducked his head so Andi could put the bridle on. Then he followed her out of the barn.

In the sunlight, Coco looked very much like an old, worn-out pony. His dark brown mane was tangled. His brown coat was dusty.

Coco touched noses with Midnight and whinnied a greeting.

"Aren't you going to clean him up?" Riley asked. He slid off Midnight's back.

"I guess," Andi said. She hurried back to the barn to get the brush and the mane comb.

Riley helped Andi brush Coco and comb out his mane. It was not easy. Andi had not taken good care of Coco. His mane was full of tangles.

"Did you really ask your mother for a horse of your own?" Riley asked as he worked.

Andi yanked on the comb in Coco's mane. "Yes. I even showed her how big I am. But she still said no."

"I didn't get a horse until I could get up on one all by myself," Riley said. He looked Andi up and down. Then he shook his head. "I don't think you can get on a horse by yourself."

Andi frowned. "I can too!"

"Try to get up on Midnight without climbing on the fence," Riley said.

So Andi tried. Once. Twice. Three times. She reached up as high as she could, but her fingers didn't even touch Midnight's mane.

She jumped as high as she could, but she still couldn't grab his mane.

Then Midnight put his head down. Quick as a wink, Andi threw her arms around Midnight's neck.

Midnight tossed his head up.

Andi went up.

Midnight turned to look at Riley.

Andi held on tight, but not tight enough. Her hands slipped, and she fell to the ground with a *thud*.

She would not be getting up on a horse by herself today.

Chapter 6

Andi's Great Idea

Andi jumped up fast. She didn't want Riley to see that she had fallen off Midnight. He might laugh. *He better not*, Andi thought. She had been laughed at too many times today already.

Riley was brushing Coco. He didn't look at Andi. He didn't laugh. Instead, he finished brushing Andi's pony and dropped the brush on the ground. Then he climbed up on Midnight.

"Come on," he said. "Let's ride."

Maybe he didn't see me fall off, Andi thought. But she knew this was not true.

Maybe—for once—Riley was not acting too big for his britches.

Andi pulled herself up on Coco and picked

up the reins. Then she jammed her heels into his sides.

"Come on, Coco," she said. "Let's go faster than a trot today."

Andi did not like to trot. Trotting made her bounce up and down. It made her slide back and forth on Coco's slippery brown back.

Andi wanted to gallop. She wanted to gallop until the wind blew her braids way out behind her back.

But Coco never galloped.

"When can I ride Midnight?" Andi asked a few minutes later. She was tired of bouncing up and down like a jack-in-the-box.

"When we get to the meadow," Riley said. "First I'll show you my new riding trick. Then you can ride Midnight."

Andi couldn't wait to get to the meadow! She gave Coco a little kick to make him go faster.

It was no use. Coco's short legs could not keep up with Midnight.

Riley waited for Andi and Coco to catch up. "So what if you're not big enough for a horse of your own?" He smiled at her. "You can ride Midnight whenever you want."

Andi pouted. "It's not the same."

"It's better than bouncing around all the time."

Riley was right about that. Anything was better than bouncing around on a pokey, hand-me-down pony.

"Can't we make Coco go faster?" Andi said at last. She shaded her eyes. The meadow looked far away. She was tired of trotting.

Just then Andi got an idea. Her best idea ever! She looked at Riley. She looked at Midnight. Then she looked at Coco.

"Riley, stop!" she hollered.

Riley stopped.

"Take Coco's reins." Andi held them out.

Riley took the reins. "What for?"

"You hold Coco's reins and gallop with Midnight," Andi explained. "Coco will have to gallop to keep up. He'll just *have* to."

It was a great plan. Why hadn't she thought of this before?

Riley looked at Coco. He looked at the reins. Then he shook his head. "I don't think this is a good idea."

"It's a *great* idea," Andi said. "Just try it one time."

Riley frowned, like he didn't want to go along with her great idea.

"Please, Riley?" Andi begged.

Riley shrugged. "Okay. One time."

Andi hugged her knees around Coco and grabbed his mane.

Riley held tightly to Coco's reins and yelled, "Giddy up, Midnight!"

Midnight took off running.

Coco took off running.

Andi laughed. Coco was galloping. Her idea was working!

For about five seconds.

All of a sudden, Coco's ears went back and he snorted. He jerked his head around. Then he jammed his feet into the soft ground and stopped.

Just like that.

When Coco stopped, Andi kept right on going—right over his head.

Thud. Andi landed on the ground with the breath knocked out of her. She groaned, but she didn't cry. She was too surprised.

Thud. Riley fell to the ground next to Andi.

"Coco pulled me off!" he yelled. "And now

Midnight is running away!" He pointed at the galloping horse.

Andi didn't say a word. She was still trying to catch her breath.

But one thing was very clear . . .

Her great idea was not so great after all.

Chapter 7

The Best Horse

Andi didn't move. She sat and watched Midnight gallop away. Her great idea had turned out to be terrible.

And now her friend Riley was mad at her.

"I'm sorry, Riley," she said. "I thought Coco would gallop if somebody made him." She let out a big sigh. "I guess he'll never be anything but a pokey old pony."

Coco looked like he didn't care. He was nibbling grass a few feet away.

Riley rubbed his hands together. "My hands hurt. I should have let go of the reins." He shaded his eyes and looked across the meadow.

Midnight was far away, under an oak tree.

He looked small—like a little black dog instead of a big black horse.

"Will he come back?" Andi asked. "Or do we have to go get him?"

"He'll come if I whistle," Riley said. He jumped up, put two fingers in his mouth, and blew out a loud whistle.

Midnight's head came up. He whinnied. Then suddenly he was galloping. Galloping back to Riley and Andi.

"Midnight is the best horse," Andi said. "He's so smart!"

"He's the best horse in California," Riley said. "Maybe in the whole world."

When Midnight stopped, Riley patted him and said, "Good boy." He climbed up on his wide, bare back. "Now I'll show you my riding trick."

Soon, Riley and Midnight were riding in a big circle around Andi. Then all of a sudden Riley stood up.

Andi gasped. Riley was standing up on Midnight. He wasn't even falling off!

Andi clapped and clapped. "Good for you! Good for Midnight!"

Riley and Midnight went around the circle one more time. Then Midnight slowed down and finally stopped.

Riley slid from his horse, pulled off his hat, and bowed.

Andi ran to Midnight. "That is the best riding trick I ever saw. Did you have to work at it a long time?"

"Every day for a month," Riley told her. "I fell off so many times that Uncle Sid almost made me stop. So don't get any crazy idea about doing that trick yourself."

"I won't," Andi said. "I just want to ride."

Riley boosted Andi up on Midnight. She picked up the reins. "I can go as fast as I want, right?"

"Yep," Riley said. "But don't take too long. I have to get back to the ranch pretty soon."

Andi promised she would come right back. She gave Midnight a little kick. "Giddy up, Midnight. Go fast!"

Midnight took off at a gallop.

Andi felt like she was flying. The grass whizzed by. The trees whizzed by.

"Faster, Midnight, faster!" she yelled.

Midnight went faster. Andi went faster.

The wind slapped her in the face. It blew her braids way out behind her back. Nothing in the whole world felt better than galloping on Midnight.

"Whee!" Andi laughed.

She rode Midnight a long way, until Riley and Coco looked like dots in the meadow.

Then she finally turned Midnight around. She did not want to go back just yet, but she had to. If she didn't, Riley might not let her ride Midnight again.

Andi didn't want that to happen. Midnight was her only chance to ride far and fast. Everybody else on the ranch was too busy to take her riding.

"That was a good, fast ride," Riley said when Andi rode up to him. "You didn't even fall off."

"I never fall off." She patted Midnight's neck. "Midnight likes me."

"Get down now. We have to go back," Riley said.

"Can't we both ride home on Midnight?" Andi begged. "I want to gallop some more."

Riley shook his head. "Coco's not big enough to keep up. And we can't just leave him here." He rubbed his hands together, like they still hurt. "I'm not going to hold his reins and drag him back, either. My hands still burn from the last time."

"Coco knows the way home," Andi said. "He can follow us."

"He looks kind of . . . kind of sad," Riley said. "All you've talked about is riding Midnight. I think Coco feels left out."

Andi looked at Coco. He was stuffing himself on grass.

"He doesn't look sad to me. He looks hungry," she said. "I promise I'll ride Coco as soon as we get back to the ranch. Then I'll brush him and put him in the corral with Midnight. Please, Riley?"

"Oh, all right," Riley said. He pulled himself up on Midnight and took the reins.

Andi sat behind Riley and held him tight. "Come on, Coco," she called to her pony. "Hurry up!"

Midnight began to trot.

Coco looked up. He gave a little whinny and began to trot too.

Then Midnight broke into a gallop and left Coco far, far behind.

Chapter 8

Missing!

Andi sat on the top rail of the corral. She was eating a sugar cookie, but it didn't taste very sweet. Nothing tasted sweet right now.

It was way past lunch, and Coco had not come home.

Andi looked out toward the meadow. She couldn't stop thinking about Coco.

"Mother is going to skin me alive," Andi whispered.

That was something the cook said to Riley when he was mad at him. "I'm going to skin you alive, boy!" Cook said when Riley knocked over a bucket of water . . . or forgot to fill the wood box . . . or dropped a pot of beans.

Being skinned alive sounded scary—even if it was only something grown-ups said when they were mad.

Andi should not have left Coco in the meadow. She should have ridden him home. If Andi was not on Coco's back making him trot fast, her pony walked as slow as a turtle.

But he should have come home by now.

"Where is he?" she asked Midnight.

Midnight blew a hot, horsey breath on Andi and snapped up her sugar cookie.

Andi didn't care. She let Midnight nibble the rest of the crumbs from her hand.

A tiny shiver went down Andi's neck. What if Coco was really, really lost? "For sure Mother will say I'm not big enough for my own horse. I'll *never* get one."

Andi sniffed back a few drippy tears. Then she thought about what she should do.

So far, nobody knew Coco was missing— not even Riley. Andi had time to find Coco and bring him home.

But how?

"I'll go back to the meadow," she told Midnight. "Maybe Coco got tired. Maybe he stopped to rest."

She rubbed the black horse on his nose. "Will you help me, Midnight? Riley said I can ride you any time I want. Now is a good time. I have to find Coco before Mother sees that he's gone."

She leaned closer to Midnight and whispered, "I don't want to be skinned alive."

Midnight shook his mane and whinnied. He looked ready to help.

Andi hopped down from the fence and found Midnight's bridle. It was hard to put the bridle on such a big horse, but Midnight helped. He put his head way down so Andi could slip it on.

Andi opened the gate. Then she climbed up on the fence and slid onto Midnight's back.

It was a long way to the meadow. This time Andi did not gallop. She made Midnight lope. A lope was faster than a trot but slower than a gallop. It was not bouncy like a trot. A lope was just right.

As Midnight loped, Andi shaded her eyes and looked for Coco. She called over and over, "Coco! Coco! Where are you?"

Coco didn't answer. No whinny. No nicker. No nothing.

The meadow was empty. Not even a

jackrabbit hopped through the grass. The sun beat down on Andi's head. It made her hot and thirsty.

Andi sniffed. Where was Coco? A few sneaky tears made her eyes wet. She rubbed them away.

Then Andi saw the oak trees. There were a lot of them. Maybe Coco was resting in the shade.

Midnight trotted across the meadow.

"Coco, are you in there?" Andi called.

Coco didn't answer.

The trees grew close together. They were too close to let a big horse like Midnight go in. The branches were prickly. He would get scratched.

So Andi slid down from Midnight's back. She tied his reins to a big branch. "Stay here," she told him. "I will be right back."

Andi took a few steps into the oak forest. It was cool and shady in there. The trees made squiggly shadows on the grass.

Just then she heard a branch snap.

"Coco?"

A deer crashed through the bushes and leaped past Andi.

"Yikes!" she yelled, very surprised. Her heart

was pounding. What other animals lived in these woods? Bears? Mountain lions? Wolves?

Andi did not want to find out. She spun around and ran back to Midnight. She couldn't look for Coco by herself. Not in these scary woods.

"I need a grown-up," Andi decided.

She didn't want to go back to the ranch. She didn't want to tell her family that she had lost Coco.

But she had to do it.

Andi untied Midnight's reins. Then she gasped.

Uh-oh!

She had slid off Midnight to look for Coco. How would she ever get back on?

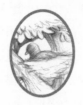

Chapter 9

Not Big Enough

Andi looked up at that big black horse. When she got off Midnight she did not think about how she would get back on. Now she was stuck.

She wasn't big enough to climb up on Midnight. And the ranch was far away—too far away to walk.

Andi felt sick in her stomach. Her heart was thumping fast. She had to think of a way to get up on Midnight!

Just then she had an idea. Maybe there was a big rock. She could climb on a rock to reach Midnight's back.

"Come on, Midnight." She yanked on the reins.

Andi and Midnight walked and walked. Pretty soon she saw a lot of big rocks. They stuck up out of the ground on a little hill. Andi found the biggest rock and climbed up. She pulled Midnight next to the rock.

"Hold still, Midnight," she said.

But Andi could not reach Midnight's back. She couldn't reach it even when she stood on her tiptoes on the biggest rock. She was just not big enough. When she tried to jump, she slipped and fell.

Ouch! Andi cried a teeny bit. Then she rubbed her eyes. "No crying," she told herself. Crying would not help her get up on Midnight.

She had to think of a new plan.

Then Andi remembered the oak trees. They were tall—much taller than Midnight. Maybe she could get on Midnight if she climbed a tree. Andi was good at climbing trees. She could do this!

Andi led Midnight back to the trees as fast as she could run. She found one that Midnight could fit under.

"Stand still," she told the horse. "Good boy. Stand really, really still."

Andi climbed the tree and kept talking
to Midnight. She sat on a branch and looked
down. It was a long drop to Midnight's back.
But she had to try it.

"Don't walk away," Andi said. "I'm going to get on you. Then we'll ride home and ask somebody to help us find Coco."

Midnight shook his mane. His tail swished. But he didn't walk away.

Andi took a deep breath. "One . . . two . . . three . . ." She dropped from her spot on the branch.

Plop! She landed on Midnight's back.

Midnight snorted his surprise, but he didn't walk away. No, he *galloped* away! He did not like surprises.

Andi tried to grab Midnight's mane, but she was not quick enough. Midnight's back was slippery. Andi slid right off—right onto the ground.

Midnight kept running.

Andi didn't yell at Midnight to come back. She didn't whistle for him. She didn't try to run after him. She just sat on the ground and let all those sneaky, drippy tears come out.

How would she get home *now*?

While she was crying, Andi was still thinking. She thought about Coco. She thought about wanting her own horse. Then she cried louder.

"Mother's right. I'm not big enough for a horse of my own. I can't even get up on one." She sniffed and tried to make the tears stop.

But she couldn't stop them. Her eyes had a lot more tears that had to come out.

"I'm sorry I was so mean to Coco," she cried. "Coco would never run off and leave me. Even if I jumped hard on his back. He's a good pony. I'm sorry I didn't take better care of him."

Andi didn't know who she was saying all these sorry words to. To God, maybe? But it wasn't nighttime. She wasn't kneeling next to her bed and saying a real prayer.

Or was this a real prayer?

Maybe she could talk to God anytime. "I'm really, really sorry," she told Him one more time.

Andi knew she had to tell Mother she was sorry too. She had to tell Coco that she really did love him.

"But first I have to find him," she told God.

Just then Andi heard a crackly sound. It was coming from inside the oak forest.

Andi jumped up and rubbed her tears away. She ran toward the noise. "Coco?"

She stopped. She did not want to go back into those woods.

The snapping and crackling grew louder. Something big was moving in the bushes!

Then Andi heard a new sound. It was a whinny.

Coco!

Andi ran into the woods. "Coco!" she shouted.

There he was, in the middle of some scratchy bushes. He looked like a mess. His reins were tangled up around the branches of a small tree. Twigs and dead leaves were stuck in his mane.

When Coco saw Andi, he whinnied. He was happy to see her.

But not as happy as Andi was to see him.

Chapter 10

Happy Birthday, Andi!

It was easy as pie for Andi to untangle Coco's reins and climb up on his back. She was so happy to see him that she leaned forward and gave him a big hug around his shaggy neck.

"I love you, Coco," she said. "Let's go home."

For once, Andi didn't care that Coco could only trot. Trotting on the back of her pony was better than walking all the way home on her own two feet. *Much* better.

When Andi was halfway home, Riley galloped up on Midnight. "What happened?" he asked. "Midnight was walking around the yard. How did he get out of the corral?"

Andi didn't want to tell Riley what happened.

She didn't want him to act too big for his britches and say, "I told you so."

But she had to tell him. It was her fault Midnight was running around loose.

After she was done telling him, Riley surprised her. "I'm glad you and Coco are friends again. And I'm glad you didn't get hurt." He smiled at her.

Andi smiled back. Hearing Riley's answer made it easier for Andi to tell Mother what had happened. It made it easier to tell Mother she was sorry.

And guess what?

Mother said the same thing Riley did.

→ ←

Andi was too excited to eat the night before her birthday.

"Tomorrow I will be six years old," she told everybody at supper.

"You've been telling us every day for the past week," Melinda said. "Are you sure your birthday is tomorrow?" She giggled.

This time Mother gave giggle-box Melinda

the warning look that said, *Don't tease your sister.*

When Andi fell asleep that night, she had only happy dreams. Dreams about a big cake with white frosting and six candles. Dreams that she blew all the candles out at the same time. Dreams that all her wishes came true.

Then right in the middle of her best dream, Andi felt the covers on her bed rip away. Her dream went *poof!* She felt cold and shivery.

Andi opened her eyes.

Chad stood over her. He had a big smile on his face.

Not funny, Andi thought. Chad was a big meanie to wake her up in the middle of her best dream. And on her birthday too!

"Give me back my covers and go away," she told him. Then she added, "Don't tease your sister!" She hoped she sounded just like Mother.

Chad did not go away. He picked her up and carried her out of her room. Holding her tight, he ran down the stairs. He didn't say a word.

When he took her outside, Andi finally asked, "Where are we going?"

"You'll see," Chad said. He pushed open the

barn door and carried her inside. "Close your eyes."

For once, Chad did not sound bossy. He sounded like he had a secret.

Andi loved secrets! So she closed her eyes.

A minute later, Chad set her down and said, "Happy birthday, little sister."

Andi opened her eyes.

Right in front of her was the most perfect baby horse Andi had ever seen. The little foal was pale gold. It had a short curly tail and a short curly mane. They were white.

Andi's heart was beating so fast she could hardly breathe.

Chad laughed softly. "I think Andi likes her birthday present, Mother."

Andi spun around. Her whole family was standing there. "This baby horse is really, really for me?" She looked at Chad. "You're not teasing me?"

Chad picked Andi up and hugged her. "Yes. She's yours. I'll help you train her. You'll have a fine horse some day."

"What are you going to name her, Andi?" Melinda asked. She was not giggling now.

Andi looked at the foal. She was creamy and golden, just like taffy candy. "I'm going to call her Taffy."

She wiggled down from Chad's arms and walked over to Mother. "But . . . you said I'm not big enough for my own horse. I have Coco. Why did you give me a horse?"

Mother smiled. "Taffy will not be ready to ride for a long, long time. She's just a baby." She put her arms around Andi. "By the time Taffy grows up, you'll be old enough to take care of her. Then Taffy will be your very own horse."

Andi gave Mother a big hug. This was her best birthday ever! Then she went over to the new foal. She reached out a finger and touched Taffy's nose.

"We're going to be best friends," she told the little horse.

Then she looked at Mother. "But Coco will always be my *first* friend."

A Peek into the Past

What would you do if your family did not own a car or a truck? Could you go to the beach? Could you visit your grandparents or your cousins or your friends? How would you carry food and other supplies home from the store?

You live during a time when almost everybody in America owns a car or a truck. But when Andi was growing up in the 1870s, there were no cars. No trucks. No minivans. For Andi's family and friends, a horse was an important animal. The horse was the "car" or "truck" of the 1800s. People rode horses to town. Horses pulled wagons. Horses pulled buggies and big carriages. They even pulled street cars (like big buses) in the city.

Most people took good care of their horses. They had to. If a horse got sick, it was just like a car breaking down. If the family horse died, it cost a lot of money to buy another one.

Children had to learn at a young age how to take good care of a horse.

Susan K. Marlow, like Andi, has an imagination that never stops! She enjoys teaching writing workshops, sharing what she's learned as a homeschooling mom, and relaxing on her 14-acre homestead in the great state of Washington.

Leslie Gammelgaard, blessed by the tall trees and flower gardens that surround her home in Washington state, finds inspiration for her artwork in the antics of her lively little granddaughter.